What's the Trouble in the Forest of Kerfubble?

By Roger & Jennifer Sulham

ISBN 978-0-9826414-9-1

Library of Congress Control Number (LCCN) 2010901923

Inkblot Press LLC

What's the Trouble in the Forest of Kerfubble?

By Roger & Jennifer Sulham

Our story begins

(for anyone who cares)

with the smallest of creatures,

a family of hares.

In their burrow they slept,

down by the lake.

Until a terrible noise

made them quiver and quake.

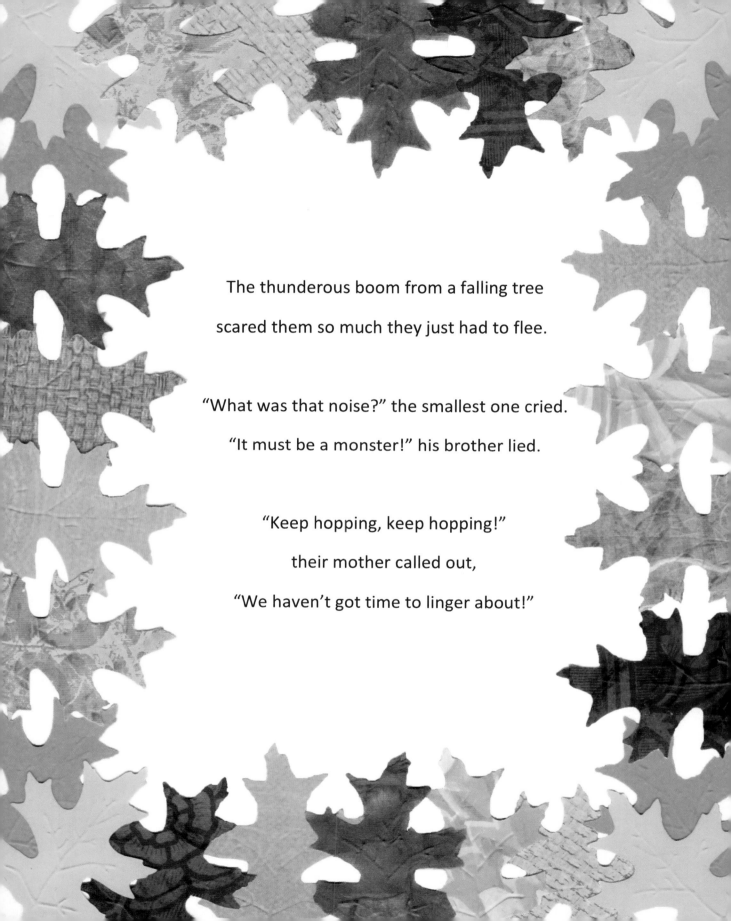

The thunderous boom from a falling tree

scared them so much they just had to flee.

"What was that noise?" the smallest one cried.

"It must be a monster!" his brother lied.

"Keep hopping, keep hopping!"

their mother called out,

"We haven't got time to linger about!"

The hares' escape caused a sudden *SPLAT!*

As they crashed right into Bobo the cat.

Now Bobo was shocked and filled with surprise.

Growing nervous from the fear in their eyes.

"Why do you flee and run on the double?

There's never any trouble here in Kerfubble."

The hares pointed back

with paws that were shaking.

"There's trouble back there!

There is no mistaking!

A terrible crash! A sure sign of danger!

It must have been caused

by a horrible stranger!"

Bobo was scared. He wanted to cry.

He had to escape. He just had to try.

He joined with the hares
in their race to depart.
"Get away from this danger!"
was the call from his heart.

Two otters were startled.
They questioned in fear.
"What's all the trouble?" then waited to hear.

"There's a monster back there
and it's headed this way!
Surely he'll eat you both up if you stay!"

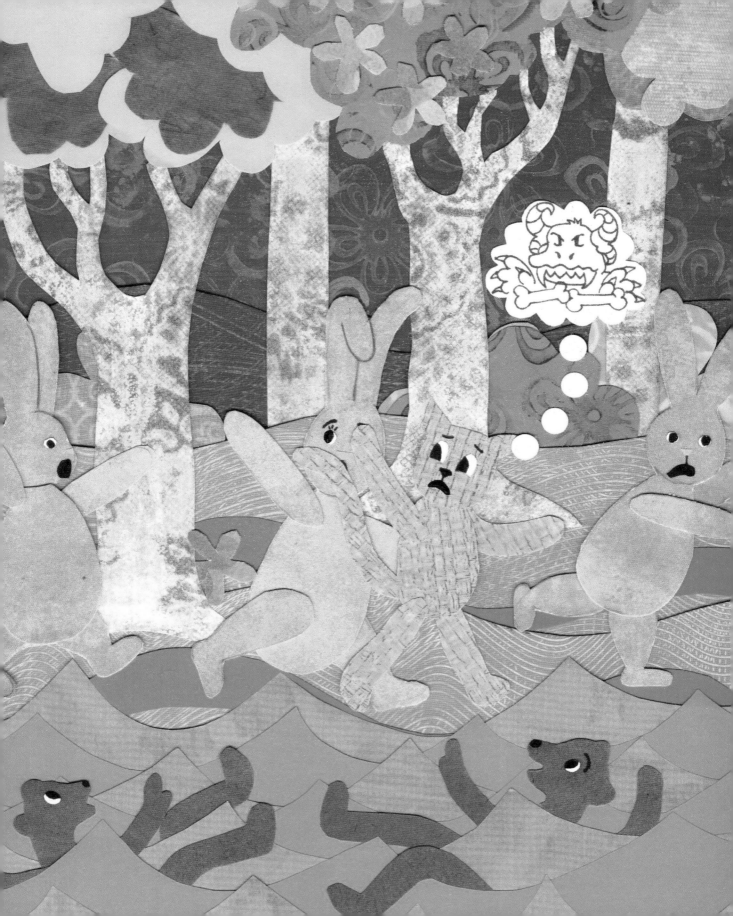

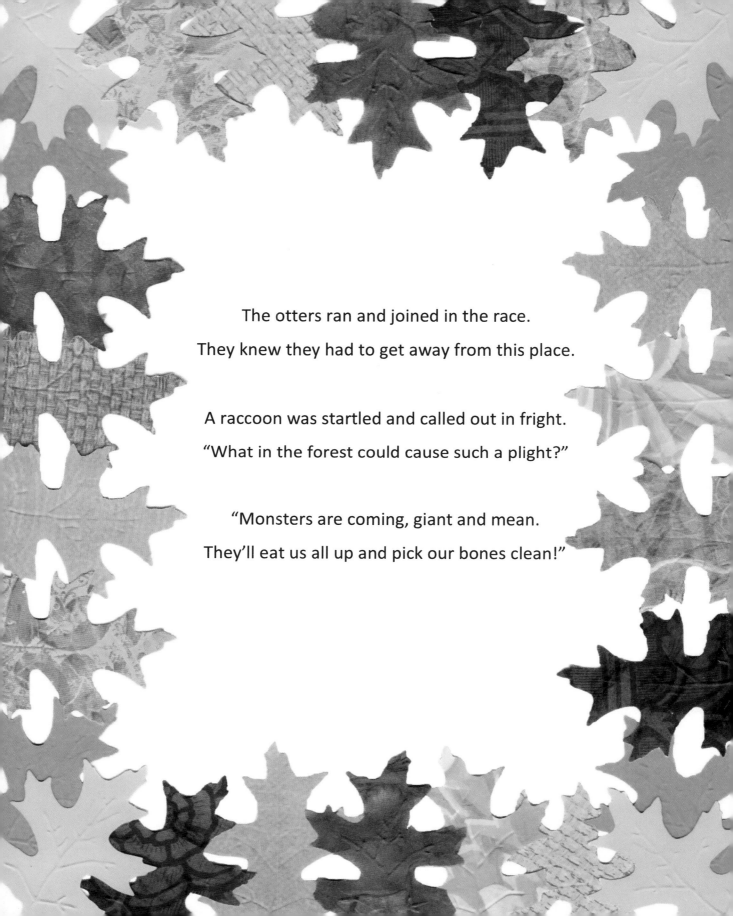

The otters ran and joined in the race.

They knew they had to get away from this place.

A raccoon was startled and called out in fright.

"What in the forest could cause such a plight?"

"Monsters are coming, giant and mean.

They'll eat us all up and pick our bones clean!"

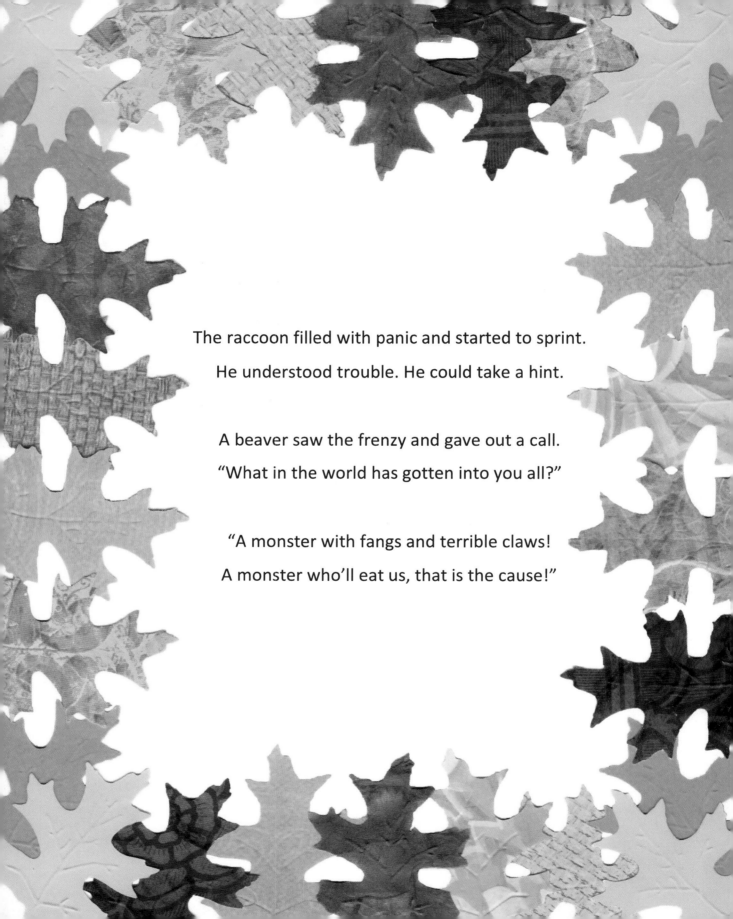

The raccoon filled with panic and started to sprint.

He understood trouble. He could take a hint.

A beaver saw the frenzy and gave out a call.

"What in the world has gotten into you all?"

"A monster with fangs and terrible claws!

A monster who'll eat us, that is the cause!"

Fox saw the commotion

and gave out a yell.

"What's going on here?

Please, you must tell."

"Terrible monsters

are out on the loose!

Horrible monsters

as tall as a spruce!"

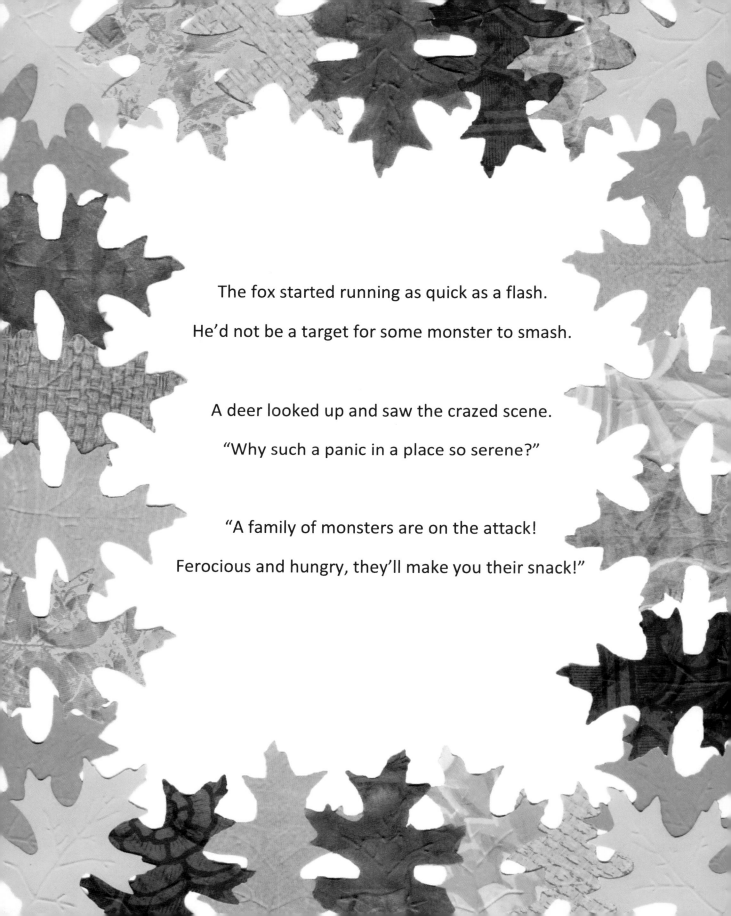

The fox started running as quick as a flash.

He'd not be a target for some monster to smash.

A deer looked up and saw the crazed scene.

"Why such a panic in a place so serene?"

"A family of monsters are on the attack!

Ferocious and hungry, they'll make you their snack!"

The deer joined the others in running away.

With their lives in such danger... how could they stay?

A bear saw them running and stood up and roared.

"What's going on here? I won't be ignored."

"A legion of monsters are hunting for meat!

Our only solution's a hasty retreat!"

The bear joined the others in running away.

Scared of becoming some monster's prey.

Dog saw the stampede and barked this demand.

"What in Kerfubble is so out of hand?"

"A horde of monsters dangerous and alarming!

An enemy so deadly there can be no disarming!"

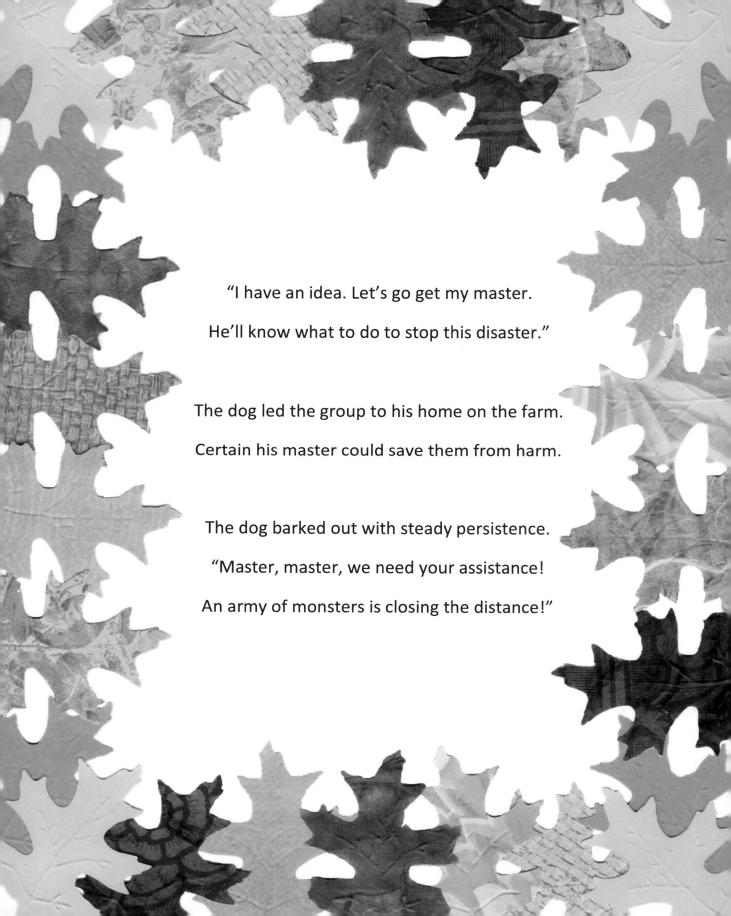

"I have an idea. Let's go get my master.

He'll know what to do to stop this disaster."

The dog led the group to his home on the farm.

Certain his master could save them from harm.

The dog barked out with steady persistence.

"Master, master, we need your assistance!

An army of monsters is closing the distance!"

The farmer questioned each one in this herd

Trying to discover what really occurred.

He led the group back to where the problem arose.

To see for themselves what he already knows.

He brought their attention to a tree on the ground,

Then let out a chuckle as they all looked around.

No monsters are coming giant and mean.

No monsters to eat you and pick your bones clean.

No family of monsters on the attack.

No family of monsters to make you a snack.

No monsters are here out on the loose.

No monsters are here as tall as a spruce.

No monsters with fangs and terrible claws.

No monsters to harm you or break any laws.

"Don't jump to conclusions," the farmer advised.

"Instead, you all should have used your own eyes.

Only the foolish follow the crowd.

Think for yourself and you'll make yourself proud."

Made in the USA
Lexington, KY
12 December 2010